D0573786

# THE ANIMALS CAME TWO BY TWO

## THE STORY OF NOAH'S ARK

# BY CHRISTOPHER WORMELL

RUNNING PRESS
PHILADELPHIA · LONDON

# For Vincent

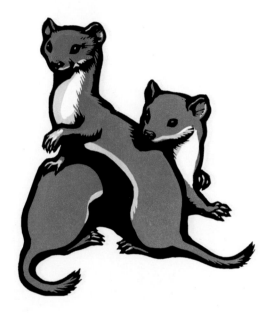

## Also by Christopher Wormell

9   8   7   6   5   4   3   2   1
Digit on the right indicates the number of this printing.

Library of Congress Control Number: 2007942769

ISBN: 978-0-7624-2718-5

Cover and interior design by Joshua McDonnell
Edited by Kelli Chipponeri
Typography: ITC Berkeley

Published by Running Press Kids, an imprint of
Running Press Book Publishers
2300 Chestnut Street
Philadelphia, PA 19103-4371

Visit us on the web!
www.runningpress.com

Long, long ago there lived a good man called Noah.

One day God spoke to Noah and told him of a great flood that would cover the whole world and drown all the creatures. He told Noah that he must save them.

"All of them?" asked Noah, wondering how he might do such a thing.

"Just two of each," replied God. "A male and a female."

"But still, there are many creatures in the world. How am I to save them?" asked Noah.

"You must build a boat," answered God. "A great ark!"

So Noah set about building a mighty ark,
large enough to carry two of every creature.
And then he began to collect them.

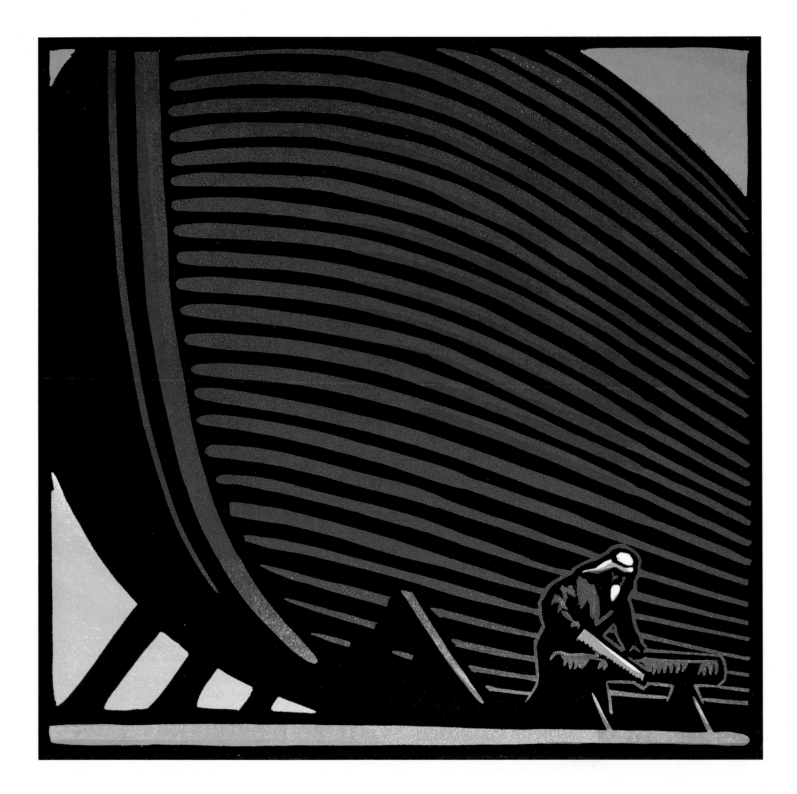

From the small…

to the large.

The tall…

to the short.

From the fat…

to the thin.

The fast…

and the slow.

From the fierce…

to the friendly.

The timid…

and the bold.

From the familiar…

to the strange.

Some were easy to collect…

while others were more difficult to capture.

At last all were gathered,
and the many creatures entered the great ark,
along with Noah and his family.

And that day it began to rain.

It rained and rained until water covered all the
land and the ark began to float. And still it rained.
It rained for forty days and forty nights until even
the tops of the highest mountains were covered.
Noah and his family and all the animals began to wonder
if they would ever again see trees or grass or flowers.

Then, on the fortieth day, the rain stopped.
Noah released a raven and said,

"Fly far and wide raven and
search the waters for dry land."

The raven did not return, so Noah released a dove.
The dove returned, but it brought no news of land.
After seven more days, Noah sent out the dove again.
This time it returned carrying an olive branch.
Noah knew that that somewhere, out in the ocean,
there must be dry land.

And so there was. For soon Noah saw an island, which grew larger by the hour. It rose higher and higher above the sinking waters for it was really the top of a high mountain. At last Noah, his family, and all the animals stepped upon dry land once more.

And though all those animals had marched onto the ark
two by two, a great many marched off three by three!

And soon the growing lands were filled
with all the animals of the world.

## HARVEST MOUSE

Mice of one sort or another are found all over the world, from forests to deserts and mountaintops to marshes. One of the smallest is the Harvest Mouse, which is only two-and-a-half inches long and weighs just one fifth of an ounce! It feeds on seeds, berries, and small insects and makes a nest of woven grasses above the ground among stems of wheat or tall grass. A male mouse is called a buck, a female a doe, and a baby mouse is sometimes referred to as a pinkie. A group of mice are a horde or even a mischief!

## ASIAN ELEPHANT

Elephants are the largest land animals in the world. The Asian Elephant can grow to be more than 10 feet tall at the arch of its back and can weigh as much as 11,900 pounds! They live in forests and grassy plains in many parts of Asia and feed mainly on grass, leaves, and shoots, using their long sensitive trunks to break off branches, and sometimes pick fruit. A male elephant is called a bull, a female a cow, and a baby a calf. A group of elephants are a herd or a parade.

## GIRAFFE

With its head up to twenty feet above the ground, the giraffe is the tallest animal in the world. Its height is due mostly to its long legs and extremely long neck—specially adapted so the giraffe can feed on leaves high up in the trees, which other grazing animals can't reach. Giraffes are found in Africa in the wide grasslands of the savannah. The male is a bull, the female is a doe, and the baby is a calf. A group of giraffes are a herd, a troop, or a tower.

## WEASEL

Standing on its hind legs the weasel isn't really short at all, but down on all fours it is. Although its body is long and slender, it has very short legs. This allows it to squeeze into the burrows of its prey—rabbits, mice, and other small rodents. Weasels are found in much of the world in woodland and hedgerow, where they nest in underground burrows. A male weasel can be called a hob, a buck, or a jack. A female weasel is known as a doe or a jill. A baby weasel is referred to as a kit. A group of weasels are a gang.

## HIPPOPOTAMUS

The hippopotamus is a very large bulky animal that lives in and around the rivers and lakes of Africa and feeds on waterside vegetation. For most of the day it wallows, almost completely submerged, in muddy water with just ears, eyes, and nostrils, which are conveniently placed on top of the head, above the surface. Hippos aren't as lazy as they appear. They are actually very good swimmers—with webbed toes—and on land they can easily run as fast as a man! A male hippo is a bull, a female a cow, and a baby a calf. A group of hippos might be called a herd, a pod, a school, or even a bloat!

## INDIAN PYTHON

Although some snakes, like the python, are quite fat around the middle, all snakes, if laid out end-to-end, are without doubt long *thin* animals. The Indian Python is one of the world's largest snakes and can be up to twenty feet long. It lives in jungles, rain forests, and mangrove swamps over much of South East Asia. The python preys upon animals as small as mice and as large as wild boar, suffocating the larger ones by encircling them with coils of its muscular body. Male and female snakes don't have particular names but a baby might be called a snakelet, a neonate, or hatchling, if it has just been born. A group of snakes are a bed, a nest, or a pit.

## CHEETAH

The cheetah is the fastest animal in the world. With its light slender body, long limbs, and high muscular shoulders, it can run at speeds of up to seventy miles per hour. It is, however, a sprinter and can only run at these speeds for relatively short distances, so with a head start and a good deal of stamina, the cheetahs' prey has some chance of escape. Cheetahs hunt the grazing animals of the African plains, as well as, birds such as guinea fowl, bustards, and young ostriches. The male and female have no particular names but the baby is called a cub. A group of cheetahs are a coalition—perhaps because they sometimes hunt as team, running in relays to chase down larger animals such as zebra.

## GALAPAGOS GIANT TORTOISE

Tortoises are slow, but so would you be if you wore a heavy suit of armour all the time like they do! Tortoises retreat into their strong protective shells when threatened by predators. They feed on a variety of vegetation and live to a great age. The Galapagos Giant Tortoise might live for more than one hundred years and can weigh as much as 600 pounds. Male and female tortoises do not have particular names, but a baby just hatched from its egg is called a hatchling. A group of tortoises are a bale.

## PEREGRINE FALCON

The Peregrine Falcon is a fearsome bird of prey. It mostly feeds on other birds diving down from above at great speed and killing them in flight. Though not very common, Peregrines are found over most of the world and nest on cliff ledges, rocky mountains, and even sometimes the sides of city buildings, which presumably they mistake for cliff faces! A male falcon is referred to as a tercel, a female is called a falcon, and a baby is dubbed a chick. A group of falcons are a cast.

## PRZEWALSKI'S WILD HORSE

The horse has been the friend and companion of man for many thousands of years, so that now almost every horse in the world is a domestic one. The only truly wild horses left are the dwindling herds of Przewalski's Wild Horses roaming the remote plains and deserts of Mongolia and Western China. Quite soon the true wild horse may well be extinct. A male horse known as a stallion, a female is a mare, and a baby is a foal, colt (male), or filly (female). A group of wild horses are a herd.

## OPOSSUM

Opossums are the only marsupials found in North America. Females carry their very young babies in a pouch on their belly—like kangaroos. They are shy nocturnal animals always avoiding confrontation. If threatened by a predator they will pretend to be dead, and even secrete an odour that makes them smell! This generally puts a predator off. A male opossum is a jack, a female is a jill, and a baby is a joey.

## LION

Lions are majestic creatures often referred to as the king of beasts. On the African plains they fear no other animal and have even been known to attack adult elephants. It is usually the females that do the hunting, working together in a small group, stalking and surrounding their prey. Male lions only join in when the prey is a large animal like a buffalo. The male is called a lion, the female a lioness, and the baby a cub. They are social animals and live in prides.

## MUTE SWAN

The swan is an unmistakable bird—a familiar site swimming in lakes and rivers all around the world—and just as familiar in the myth, legend, and art of many cultures. The Mute Swan is a European species which, unlike the Whistling or the Trumpeter for example, is silent—hence its name. They do, however, hiss when angry! Swans feed on aquatic vegetation, dipping their heads below the surface and using their long necks to reach the river bottom. They build large twiggy nest and pairs often bond for life. A male swan is known as a cob, and female a pen, and a baby a cygnet. A group of swans are referred to as a bevy, a game, a herd, or a team.

## PLATYPUS

The platypus is a very strange creature—almost like a mixture of other animals. It has the sleek streamlined body of an otter and a bill and webbed feet like a duck! As you may have guessed, it spends much of its time underwater, where it feeds on crustaceans, aquatic insects, and larvae. Platypuses are found in the lakes and rivers of Eastern Australia and Tasmania, where they live in riverbank burrows. The males and females have no particulars names, nor is there a name for a group of platypuses, but a baby is called a puggle.

## DODO

The Dodo was a large flightless bird that once lived on the islands of Mauritius in the Indian Ocean. It fed on fruit, nested on the ground, and had no fear of predators, because there were none. At least there were no people on the islands then and no animals that ate Dodos. Alas, there came a time when passing sailors discovered the islands, and being flightless and fearless the Dodos were very easy to catch and turn into roast dinners! By the late 17th century there was not a single Dodo left. They were related to doves and pigeons. The males, females, and their young do not particulars names.

## HEDGEHOG

Hedgehogs are not so easily caught. They have a coat of spines and can curl up into a tight spiky ball. Many a young fox has been left with a very sore mouth after puzzling over how to make a meal of this prickly morsel! Hedgehogs are found in Europe, Africa, Asia, and New Zealand, where they root around, grunting and snuffling like little pigs. They live in woodland and hedgerow, where they search for worms, insects, snails, or berries. The male is called a boar, the female a sow, and the baby a piglet or pup. A group of hedgehogs are an array.

Chris Wormell is a leading English wood engraver. Inspired by the works for Thomas Bewick, he took up wood engraving in 1982, and has since illustrated several books in addition to his work in the fields of advertising, design, and editorial illustrations.

Long before Christopher became a wood engraver he was taught lino-cutting by his father, mainly for the mass production of Christmas cards. Around Christmastime the Wormell household became something of a cottage industry with Christopher and his brothers and sisters producing handmade cards by the hundreds.

His first book for children, *An Alphabet of Animals,* started a series of simple, lino-cut illustrations for his son Jack, and eventually grew into a book that took the Graphics Prize at the Bologna International Book Fair in 1991and spawned a sequel, *The New Alphabet of Animals.* Most recently, Christopher has received acclaim for his animal counting book *Teeth, Tails, & Tentacles,* which was named a *New York Times* Book Review Best Illustrated Children's Book, an American Library Association Notable Book, and a Kirkus Reviews 2004 Editor's Choice, among other. Some of Christopher's other children's book credits include *Mowgli's Brothers, Blue Rabbit and Friends, Blue Rabbit and the Runaway Wheel, Animal Train, Off to the Fair, George an the Dragon, Two Frogs, In the Woods, The Big Ugly Monster and the Little Stone Rabbit,* and *Swan Song,* a collection of poems by J. Patrick Lewis about extinct animals.

He lives in London with his wife and three children.